THE UNCERTAIN FUTURE OF US

SOUVIK BOSU ROY

Copyright © Souvik Bosu Roy
All Rights Reserved.

Contents

Acknowledgements

I would like to thank my late mother Kanika Bosu Roy whose comments and suggestions were of inestimable value for my study. Special thanks also go to my late grandmother Sandhya Bosu Roy, my woman Archita Das, my brothers Avradeep Das and Avik Ghosh and all the Facebook friends who encouraged me to write a story who provided technical help and sincere encouragement. I would also like to express my gratitude to my family for their moral support and warm encouragements. Finally, I would like to thank Dhruv Kumar Danda for helping me out in almost every financial problem and encouraging me all the time.

ONE

EPISODE-1

Today is June 6, 2021. I'm just 8 days away from turning to 21 years. You're younger than me, doing your college degree. We met when I was a jobless boy who just passed out from college. After 6 months, I got a job but it's still not enough for me due to the excessive financial load of my family. We used to sit under the starry night sky thinking about our future, about the uncertainty of us lasting together forever. What's going to happen if I don't get a high salary job or a settled career, what if you think that I couldn't give you the luxury comfort, you are given by your father for all these years? Everyone tells that if there is love, nothing can give more comfort than that. But in reality, we all know that after a certain period of time, we all get over this fact. That's when the gap increases, the toxicity increases, every beautiful thing in the world shatters. We both have already imagined our future though. Even though, these are all our imaginary scenes of our future, we feel happy thinking of that but after a few minutes, the fear of "What if it doesn't happen?" comes and all of a sudden the bloom of happiness fades away. We were walking down the empty streets, not knowing where we were going but later on your phone ring with auntie's call and it hit our less used brain that it's already 10 P.M. and we have to return to our respective homes where a bag of abuses were waiting for us. I got to the last train from Sealdah Railway Station at 11:40 P.M. Baba is calling me for the 12th time and by each call the voice is getting louder and louder with some typical Bengali slangs. After reaching home, as usual we listened to every piece of shits, addressed to us. We are used to call or text over the nights. We were never the kind of couples doing sexting or telling each other how much we love each other in every minute or anything like that. Every night, we talk about us along the unwanted possibility of what if this is going to be the last call? We do over think the little things and that shit hits hard. Every time, I asked her "What if this don't work out in the future, we will have nothing but a black hole of trauma. You know what, the over thinking and the thoughts of uncertainties can ruin it all. We had thought about that too. But we do what we do. Some things can't be controlled if the other things are forcing your mind to do so. I know, we are very young but what if we can't make it in the future? What if the tragedy of our lives ruins it all and the climax of our 'US' ends with "No, we can't be together anymore, we are done".

TWO
EPISODE-2

Tomorrow is June 14, 2021. It's my birthday. And right now it's 7.30 P.M. in the evening of June 13, 2021. Me and Sreyashi had planned to celebrate this evening together with a bottle of Magic Moments Green Apple and will try to forget the bad thoughts for a while. And guess where I am now? Bagbazar Ghat. Sitting next to the last stair up from the water level. Observing the flow of the river, lighting a cigarette with the dried tears on my cheeks. Our plan went into veins after her exam results out and she found that she failed the exam. Her parents locked her in her room and gave all the credits to our relationship for her result. It was not a blame to be honest. It is what it is. She failed because of our relationship, because of my over thinking which I transmitted into her brain too with my illogical "What If's". People advice to go with the flow but what if the flow outflows you and your situations? Again, I'm over thinking this. I don't have a single friend whom I can describe all these. She is my only friend. Maybe, this is why people tell you to have some friends but what if those friends ditch you with a mask of well wishers on their faces. Fuck it, I'm okay. I just need some time to settle my mind over all these slide shows in my mind. But do you know what? She neither blamed me nor our relationship. I don't know why this crazy woman values a shit like me so much? Yes I'm lucky to have her. But am I really being selfish nowadays? I know I'm looking for my happiness and making her sacrifice her dreams. We never wanted this type of relationship. I texted her right at the moment when I was thinking about these.

Me: Oi Sreyashi, are you okay? I'm sure you will say yes even if you're not. I have something to ask you? I know this is not the right time to ask you this but still if we don't think about this right now, we may end up by ruining everything.

Sreyashi: Why do I need to be not okay? You're with me, right? And that's all I want.

Me: Okay, so listen, can we get a break for a month or at least a few days?

Sreyashi: What? I can't understand what break you're talking about.

Me: I meant about our relationship, can we take some time of break to know if I'm the reason behind all of your problems which are increasing from last few months?

Sreyashi: Ohh, Accha!

Me: Yes, just listen to me once.

The call cut with a voice of crying in silence.

Did I make a mistake? Am I really a dumb or am I over thinking it again?

The waves just touched my knees and that suddenly struck a hit in my mind. I don't have any cigarettes left in my pocket or bag.

THREE

EPISODE-3

God please discharge me from this hell of problems. It's the 50th call I'm placing hoping that this time her phone may be switched on but getting the same "the number you're trying to reach is currently switched off" tune reflected. I am everything for her, her home, healer of her mental health, everything that a person wants. No I never said these; she believes these even I don't want her to feel like nothing is more important than me even if it's her career. And today I have hurt that person more than anything else could. I don't love myself how much she does. Maybe I don't deserve her. Every memory of us is flashing inside my head and it's hurting like someone hitting my head with a hammer of Thor. I never thought this birthday would start like this and who knows, if there is something worse that is waiting for me. My body is getting colder minute by minute. I can't even visit her home right now. It's already 11.30 P. M.

11:50 P. M.

Some of my WhatsApp contacts who only recall me every year on my birthday. And now for the last 2 years, I just give a reply to one of them and copy paste the rest of them. I just light up a cigarette from the box I just bought while returning home devastated. I'm not bothered whether anyone else wishes me or not. I'm just waiting for her to call, knowing she won't wish this time. It's 11.59 P. M. and with all the worst circumstances hovering in my mind clears when my phone rings. I just threw the cigarette away to pick the call assuming it would be her for sure. But.......

It was one of my WhatsApp contacts, who I had heard has a crush on me. I declined the call with all the waves of tears coming out. Then at 12 AM of June 14, 2021, her text came.

Sreyashi: Happy Birthday. Enjoy your day how you want. Stay happy

Me: Fuck my birthday, where were you? Have you eaten? Please talk to me for a while. I can make you understand everything I wanted to say at that time. Wait I'm calling you, please pick up the phone for once.

She went offline giving me a dark night of silence.

I called her but again "the number you're trying to reach is currently switched off".

FOUR

EPISODE-4

I didn't want to close my eyes for the night but when I opened my eyes, the sunrays from the window were wishing me 'Happy Birthday' triggering my eyes. I saw my phone was lying on the floor, the ashes of the cigarettes spreaded all over the bed from the ash tray beside my bed. I quickly plugged in the charger to my phone and switched it on. And when the phone got switched on, some random messages from the WhatsApp chats came to irritate me as always. Then a message came notifying me that Sreyashi had called me 20 times when my phone was switched off. Why am I such a dumbass? I didn't pick up the call. Everyone in this world wants to start a new day with a strong coffee and a kiss on the forehead and here I'm starting my special day with my over thinking. What if she called me due to some problem? What if she wanted me to meet her? What if she wanted to talk over every single thing that is bothering us for such a long time? I instantly tried to call her and this time the phone wasn't switched off but the ring continues and then "The number you're trying to call is unable to take your call right now" and it constantly happened for the 15th time. There was no other option for me rather than going to her home to meet her and I did so. It was a 30 minutes train ride from my house to her house. The impractical thoughts, the impossible things were haunting me continuously. I reached her home, pressing the bell for the second time with a fear of getting slammed by her parents due to her results. Aunty opened the door with tears in her eyes. I was half dead at that moment thinking what if the impractical thoughts which were haunting me turned into reality? I asked her softly with a fear to hear something I wasn't ready for. She told me that Sreyashi didn't eat last night, was crying all the night and when they went to wake her up, she was not in her room. She has left nothing to trace her. I assured aunty to get calm down; I'll take her back to home. I turned back and ran towards the railway station. I wasn't sure where she was but if I have love her so much and if we have created the bonding between us, then she will be where I'm heading to.

Any guesses?

Our **US** destination 'Bagbazar Ghat', the place where we first met, the place where we sit whenever some problems hit our lives. I reached Bagbazar Railway Station and ran to every ghat in that area searching her but she was not there. Then where was she? If she is not here, then she could go only to that place, the silent valley of dead peoples in the center of Kolkata, 'Park Street Cemetery'. At last my assumptions got correct. I found her at the cemetery, facing towards the grave of her grandfather whom she loves the most before he passed away in 2016. I got close to her and touched her shoulder. She hugged me instantly when she saw me there beside her and started crying and saying "Please don't leave my like dadu" and I couldn't take out any words after that. I hugged her and cried too and told her that "I'm not going anywhere, my mad woman". We talked for a while and the ghost of taking a break taken down by her love. I assured her that nothing going to happen if she returns to her home, no one is going to ask her anything about where she was, why she left in the morning. And after consoling her with all the assurances, we left the cemetery and took the road to reach the nearest metro station. We're happy again, blushing and smiling and looking at each other like we are always used to. But I had full confidence on my bad luck that the happiness wouldn't last long and a sudden boooooooommmmm....

FIVE

EPISODE-5

June 14th, 11.30 P.M.

The best ever bithday of mine is coming to an end with something no one ever expect it to be.

We are at the hospital. Everyone except me is waiting for the doctor to come out with an update from the OT room. That crazy girl is crying heavily and me lying unconsciously on the bed of the OT. No, I'm not dead yet. Do you remember that booommmm? We were crossing the signal holding each others' hand, glancing at each other happily. A rushing bike came and wished me the best birthday wish by hitting me from the side and ran away. Instantly I realized what the hell of pain really is, there was no sense of the right leg in my body but most luckily I saved her from getting hit. It was my win to do something for her in my life.

At last the doctor came out from the OT room and called my father to tell the news (my hands are shaking right now) the news that his son will not be capable to stand or walk or run like a normal human being as the bone marrow of his son is damaged heavily. There was no chance for me to use my leg anymore, not even the way the movies show. It's real life. A family which was dependent on me for the financial side is now done with their lives. Their only son who got the job just 1 year ago after being jobless is again a jobless man who can do nothing, literally nothing. A burden for his family. I have already ruined the lives of me and my family but I will not ruin that girl's life who loves me more than herself. I can't betray her by staying with her for the rest of our lives. It was the 3rd day in the hospital after the surgery. Trust me, I didn't cry for even once. I was not inside me.

On the 3rd morning's visiting hours, I saw her coming inside my hospital room. Is that the same girl I met 3 days ago? No, it can't be. Is this happened because of me? Looking at her felt like she is more unwell than me.

I asked: Hi, Did something happen to you?

She didn't answer

Me: Am I audible to you? Have you eaten? Or as always you starved for the sorrow of us not talking for the day?

Sreyashi: Am I looking in a sarcastic mood to you?

Me: No, I just told what you usually do and it's real.

Sreyashi: Look, don't try to make me laugh. I just came here to let you know that we can't stay together anymore. You can judge me, assume whatever you want but we are done.

Me: Am I hearing right? You're saying this? Seriously? Okay, I will talk to you once I return home. Will it be fine for you?

Sreyashi: We can't meet anymore. Sorry for everything. I ruined your life.

Me: No you didn't. You have nothing to do with it.

She left the room and the world of over thinking hurt me again. And this time all the over thinking is turning into reality. Do I assume every bad thing is coming in my life?

SIX

EPISODE-6

I have been discharged from the hospital and returned to my home by sitting on a wheel chair. Great! The boy who loved to play football so much is on the wheel chair and will never be able to play football. For the last few days, I spent my time in hospital thinking about the reason why she made this decision where she never said anything close to that. I called her to let her know that I'm at home and if she can come to talk over everything that's happening between us.

She picked up the call and said roughly: Why are you calling me? I told you not to contact me anymore, right?

Me: Hey, what happened? I'll not call you ever but I need to know the reason for this treatment you're giving to me. This Sreyashi is completely unknown to me than whom I loved.

Sreyashi: Loved? Now you know the reason. You loved me and now you don't, right?

Me: I don't want to say that. I request you to please meet me once and clear everything, after that you do whatever you want to. I'll not say a single word. But please once.

Sreyashi: You want me to hurt you again? You're on the wheel chair right now due to my nonsense. You promised maa to find me and take me back to my home and doing that your life changed and I couldn't do a single shit. We both could have died, we both could have on the wheel chairs if you didn't try to save me from getting hit by that bustard's bike. And what did I do for you? Just see you lose your walking capability, lose your job, lose your dreams, your family crying for their son and their future. I had given you a nightmare as your birthday gift. I ruined everything. Even though you're not happy. Do you want me to kill you now as that's the only thing I haven't done to you. If you haven't loved me, your life will not be ruined like it is right now. You deserved a girl who is more mature than me. I'm just a useless, immature moron.

Me:

You're the best

for me. You're just over thinking it. Listen, It's my fate that I'm on this shitty wheel chair right now. Don't blame yourself for all of these. Please come once to me, I'll be a little happy to see you once. Please...

She cut the call.

SEVEN

EPISODE-7

It's 8 P.M. in the evening. She didn't come. It never happened before. So, is she really changed or she's over thinking it and blaming herself for my situation? How can I fix this mess? I can't even stand so there's no chance for me to go to her house and talk to her. I don't know what's wandering in her mind. What if she hurt herself due to her over thinking. I couldn't be able to save her and if that happens the guilt of that will haunt me everywhere. No, she won't do that.

On 9.30 P.M. she called me. I thought the over thinking might be less now.

But it was not her, it was auntie's voice over the other side of the call, crying bitterly and telling me to talk to her and make her understand that she is wrong.

I asked her: Aunty, why you're crying? What happened? And where is Sreyashi? She didn't come today.

Aunty: Thank God for that. If she had gone to meet you, no one knows what she would have done on the way.

Me: What? I can't understand. Where is she?

Aunty: She is sleeping. The doctor has injected him Haloperidol injection. She had tried to jump from the balcony. She had tried to commit suicide. She is thinking that she is the guilty of your current situation and that's why she wants to give her the punishment by doing these. Due to god's grace, your uncle saw her and pulled her back. Otherwise, we don't know what will happen?

(I was numb at that moment, a continuous beep all over my mind and ears)

Aunty: Son, can you come once? We'll send a car to come. If I need to talk to your parents, I will. But she needs you and we can't take risk of her to got to you. I know, I may sound selfish to you but you might understand why I'm telling this. You know her very well, you know how sensitive she is.

Me: I will go. I will talk to my parents. Tell me the time, I'll be ready.

Aunty: Okay. Thanks babu. I'm cutting the call now, otherwise she may wake up. I believe in you and I know you can make her stable as before. We'll be always grateful to you.

She cut the call and I start thinking.

EIGHT

EPISODE-8

It's raining heavily tonight. Maybe god is in tears seeing us. I've been thinking only about her from the time auntie cut the call. How can I make her believe that she is not the reason behind my crippled state? Holy shit! The rain is reminding me of that evening we danced on the street while returning home. We were completely wet in the rain. We knew we will get tremendous abuses at our homes for our nonsense but we didn't care and the next day she got high fever.

To be honest, it's actually not funny. She has an issue of Neurogenic Fever due to an accident when she and her dadu were travelling in Delhi by an auto in 2015 and the auto got in an accident with a bus and her head affected dangerously, the auto driver was spot dead and her dadu was taken to the hospital but the doctor told that he was dead too. Sreyashi was been in a trauma from that time. That's why her parents shifted from Delhi to Kolkata, they thought that the fear or trauma their daughter was suffering might end here. From that time, whenever she falls in fever, there always a tension of her parents that she might recall those nightmares again. Although, she was able to move on from that trauma or may be just for some time. And now, the person, she thought would never leave, whom she loved the most is again got into an accident and she was there this time too. So, is this happening due to that? Oh shit! I have to talk to her tomorrow as early as I can.

I spent the night sleeplessly. My brain isn't working. I pushed her to that trauma again but I tried to save her. Oh god! Help me please.

The next morning at 9 o'clock, the car came. Baba had gone with me. We reached to her home by 10.30 A.M. as the roadways are always longer than the railway tracks and the traffic jam of Kolkata is also there. We saw uncle standing outside their gate. He helped baba to take me down from the car. When we entered into her room, we saw the doctor standing there and maybe he was waiting for me to come.

She was sleeping. Tears rolled out from my eyes seeing her like that, tied hands to the bed with ropes. I was going to untie her immediately when the doctor stopped me. He took us outside of her room to discuss further. He told us not to react by his words before listening it all. We all agreed by keeping a rock on our chests.

Doctor: Listen, I have checked the reports of her brain. I just got to know about that previous trauma of her from you today. I don't know if you ever heard about this but as per the reports, she is suffering from a condition known as "POST-TRAUMATIC STRESS DISORDER (PTSD)" can sometimes occur after you experience a life-threatening event or witness a death. To be very honest, there is no cure of PTSD in this world but we can bring her back to normal life by psychotherapy, meditations but to make her do those we have to ensure spending time with her, trying to divert her mind from any type of sorrows, over thinking, suicidal thoughts or anything else that can turn her down. I know this won't be easier but we don't have any options other than that. Hey boy, you love her right? And she got to this because of your accident, right? I believe if she loves you the most, it's you and only you who can be the most effective bridge for her to back to her normal life. You can do it. You can save her. We all are with you.

I was stunned and numb. I was not good at science but no one needs to know science to understand what he is talking. What if I can't do that? What if she doesn't get well? What if.....fuck it. I'll try every single thing to get her out from this disease. I love her and I will give my 200% efforts for her. Even if I fail, I will know that I have tried and the guilt might get less though I know it won't. I will be forever guilty for both of our lives.

I told doctor: I'll give my everything to bring her out from whatever she is suffering from. I promise you everyone. And if I fail, I'll not be here too.

Everyone was looking at me like I'm the God's child angel for them to whom their every emotions, their destinies were lying ahead. I took my eyes up and gave a fake smile to them and went to her room by handling the wheels of my wheel chair with a fake smile on it wiping off the tears.

NINE

EPISODE-9

A few glances at her, it's making me more and worse in my head. I was there, so that she didn't return to this state and now it's because of our relationship, she is again in that state. To be very honest and it's obviously my personal opinion but I don't believe in god. Maybe that 'god' thing never supports me, that's why. I'm waiting for her eyes to open but it is striking my mind too that the doctor told me not to feel her any sense of guilt but she will see me sitting on the wheel chair every time, I can't change that, it's not in my hands. So? What if she starts to recall those nightmares again seeing me like this. I'm unable to think about any of the positive possibilities. But I have to. Every time I try to think about something positive, all the research on Google about **PTSD** I did in the past hours was sending the positives far away. As per studies, the presence of psychotic symptoms in patients suffering from **POST-TRAUMATIC STRESS DISORDER (PTSD)** may represent an under-recognized and unique subtype.

PTSD has 5 stages -

- Impact or Emergency Stage

- Denial/ Numbing Stage
- Rescue Stage (including Intrusive or Repetitive stage)
- Short-term Recovery or Intermediate Stage
- Long-term reconstruction or recovery Stage

At last she was awake. She was looking at me, in my wheel chair. I can feel the anxiety in her eyes. She is about to cry and fill the room with her tears. I quickly hugged her and held her until she felt comfortable. I was not on the side of the people who think injecting a sleep injection to make them stable is suffering from something like Sreyashi. Rather, we can make them feel comfortable with us, spend time with them, let them understand how much beautiful life is waiting for them ahead. Despite these things Sreyashi is suffering from, she is a very playful girl, and wants to enjoy every single moment. She told me not to wait for the right moments, to live every moment of our lives. She is a big fan of SRK and used to always say **"Haso, Jiyo, Muskurao, Kya Pata Kal Ho Na Ho"** And today it seems that she may have known it was all coming. She has stopped crying now.

She asked me: Are you better now? Are you still feeling the pain badly?

I didn't let her understand what pain I'm feeling, not only in my legs but in my heart and brain too and said,

Me: Yes, I'm far better now. The doctor has told Baba that if someone agrees with a bone marrow transplant, I will be better like before. (Though these were all my self made thoughts I told using the name of the doctor, it's temporary but I don't have any other options right now) And How're you? I heard that you had tried to jump out of your balcony? Should I expect these types of nonsense things from you, my woman? Giving up isn't the solution, try to fix everything by being present there nah! Even being a cripple, I didn't give up, I could have. Isn't it? But did I? I lived for you, for my family, for US, the uncertain future of us.

● 21 ●

TEN
EPISODE-10

She heard it with all of her consent. I don't know how much did she understood. She faced to the balcony of her room and stared for 15 minutes without speaking a single word out from her mouth. I started to sing a song which I used to sing for her whenever we do over thinking about our relationship.

Oh! I'm Obsessed
With The Way Your Head Is Laying On My Chest
How You Love The Things I Hate About Myself
That No One Knows But With You, I See Hope Again
Oh! I'm A Mess
When I Over think The Little Things In My Head
You Seem To Always Help Me Catch My Breath
But Then I Lose It Again
When I Look At You, That's The End

She melted in my arms and requested me to stay there. I did because I promised myself to do whatever she feels good. I stared at her all the night long. She is the most beautiful girl I have ever seen. I'm blessed that she got faith in me and myself. I thought, I'm not enough to be loved by someone but she made me believe in myself. I wish this uncertainty of our love end and I get to spend all my life with her. The love between us never gets faded away. Now I'm sure there's no one who can make me happier than me. And I will keep her trust on me. We both will be better than how we are right now. We'll never be perfect, to be honest, no one ever can. We'll live together will all our imperfections.

The starry night, the winds passing away, the full moon, the fireflies everything was reminding me all our dates, all our memories spent together. All the gifts were here and there in her room. I found a letter beside her bed. I unfolded it. Maybe she had written it before attempting suicide that day. The letter was all about how much she love me, how much I means to her and the over thinking, regrets, guilt's she was having. I put down the letter where it was. I don't want her to know that I've read it.

She is sleeping peacefully, smiling in her dreams; maybe she is dreaming about the US, we were used to be. Oh shit! I've to go to toilet now, but how? No one is here to put me on the wheel chair beside me and I can't wake her up to do so. Let's try a little bit. I have to manage it on my own. I'll write the rest of my each and every emotions getting back to the room from the best thinking zone in the world. I'm putting the first rose here you've given on our first date which is now dried and few of the petals of it are left but for me it's still the fresh red rose you've given with all of your love.

This was the last line of his diary that he left for us.

Hi, I'm Sreyashi. It's 12 A.M. of 14th June 2022. It's his birthday. I have found his diary last year and had promised myself to read it on the start of his next birthday. I was given sleeping pills at that night of 20th June of 2021 due to my anxiety issues. The night, he wrote the last few pages of his diary. As per my parents and the doctors he fell down from the stairs while going to the toilet at that night and never wake up. You might have thinking how I'm writing this as I was a patient of PTSD. Yes, I'm fine now. His words from that day made me understood how much beautiful our lives are, we just have to find the beautiful things, he lived for me, for the US when he had the real reason to give up but he never tried. And now I'll live for him, for the US. He also sent me a voice note where he sang "Hum rahe ya na rahe kal, kal yaad ayenge ye pal" and he hadn't lied. I was listening to all his favorite songs on loop. I'm crying but will never do anything that might hurt her soul. Nowadays, uncle lives with us after his son's death. Now, I've two father figures and they both love me like their own daughter. To the love of my life, I'll always cherish the memories we both have shared together and I'll be your woman forever and will prove that "Forever isn't a lie even if we both can't met". I blew the candles over the cake I had made myself today and wished him "Happy Birthday, Champ. You won everything. The love between us is never going to be uncertain anymore. In another life, I'll be your woman and will never leave you anywhere."

Dear lovers, love your loved ones, life is such unpredictable. Don't waste your period of life by over thinking, having trust issues between your 'US'. Believe in your love. Be in love. Search for the good things and live your life to the fullest.

I'm closing the diary now forever and will keep it forever until I die. Till then, it's not a good bye, it's just see you later.

THE END